SWOLE: CHEST DAY

Published and written by: Golden Czermak
3rd Edition

WARNING: This is a **short story** written for mature readers. It is pure escapism, containing adult themes, coarse language, erotic sexual situations, male-male sex, and nudity.

ACKNOWLEDGEMENTS

This work would not be possible without such great support from readers and others in the book community.

Thank you to the #AITC crew, specifically Kim, Donna, and Stephanie, for helping me realize the proper use of a tanning booth.

Special thanks to all my gym bros out there for helping inspire the premise for this erotic short story series. I'll leave it at that, so everyone can ponder what exactly I meant by it.

SWOLE

CHEST DAY

CHAPTER 1

AN UNEXPECTED MEETING

TRENT CASSIDY WAS A PRETTY smug guy on the best of days and an unequivocal asshole on the worst of them. One of the few things that could make him even more dickish was if someone managed to wake the bearded bastard too early on one of the few mornings he could sleep in.

That happened to be this very morning, just past three o'clock.

Jesus Christ Jared; you klutz! Trent's thoughts screamed while his eyes flung open to the sounds of clashing metal coming from elsewhere in the house. *For fuck's sake, I told you I didn't have any clients this morning.*

Tempted to bolt out of bed so he could give his roommate a piece of his mind, the comfy mattress and a crumpled strip of white sheet were enticing enough to keep Trent still. Jared was getting a rare second chance to avoid a verbal bombardment.

Green eyes adjusting to the dimness of cool light cast by a single nightlight on the far wall, Trent took in his bachelor-like bedroom. There was an array of straight-lined furniture clad in leather and chrome, and for the few minutes he looked around, there was no noise other than the faint hum of air from the vents. Pleased that he could return to sleep, he rubbed a hand through his thick, black hair, and his eyelids became heavy. However, they didn't manage to get all the way closed.

A thunderous avalanche of crashing noise came, and the sheets flew off, Trent shooting to his feet in an instant. Now pissed off that he was wide awake, he stormed out of the room and down a short hallway.

"Jared!" Trent spat, rounding the base of some stairs. "What the hell are you…"

He stopped mid-sentence; Jared wasn't there to hear any of his tirades. Instead, a stranger was standing in *his* kitchen. Not only that, he was filling one of *his* plastic shaker cups with water from *his* fridge.

Trent's frustration rose.

This part of town is going to shit, he thought, recalling stories of similar things happening, especially at spring break.

Strangely, the man hadn't noticed Trent yet, so he took a moment to observe the vagrant. He was a short guy, about five-foot-six, give or take a couple of inches. Dressed in joggers and a loose white tee, his much smaller frame was evident; Trent was assured that he could take the man down if he needed to.

"Hey bum, parties don't start until Monday, near the beaches," Trent said, raising his voice. He wasted no time balling up his fists, slamming them against a nearby table. "Who the hell are you?"

The man flinched at the unexpected noise, dropping the full cup onto the floor. Water went everywhere as the container bounced, and his light blue eyes widened like saucers to stare at the veritable mallets hanging on either side of Trent's body.

Wow, not so much a bum then, Trent's mind wandered as he admired the young, smooth features in front of him. *Play time.*

"Listen here dude: if you don't answer me," Trent carried on, taking a weighty step forward, "I'm going to make sure you lick every drop of that up after I get done beating the shit out of..."

"W-wait!" the man stuttered, watching Trent's lips curl and his abs tense. "I'm n-not here to s-steal a-anything!"

The tone of Trent's voice was menacing like his muscles and the stranger visibly perturbed.

"Looks like you're stealing my water. So, answer me!" Trent demanded, getting even closer. His heart was beating fast with enjoyment. "Who. Are. You?"

"I-I'm just v-visiting," he replied, nervously raising his arms in defense.

Trent strode around a low bar counter, took a couple more steps, and stopped within inches of the outsider, crossing his arms. The stranger's eyes lined up just above Trent's furry chest, but they didn't stay put, roaming all over his shirtless body.

"That's not what I asked you," Trent replied, slow and deep.

The man took a step backward, stopped before he was startled by the chilly fridge door. Up close Trent was a tank, much bigger than he was… everywhere.

"J-Jared!" said the man, his words stammering after a hard gulp. As he spoke, it felt like his heart had moved into his throat. "I-I'm friends with Jared! You know him, right? Jared Hughes?"

Fuck, Trent thought, the look sweeping over his face a mix of satisfaction and disappointment. He was hoping to fuck with the guy longer since being roused from a good sleep. There were still other ways to get paid back, and Trent was going to make sure he got it.

"Jared, eh? So, are you his fuck buddy or something?" Trent asked bluntly, tilting his head. "After all, it is spring break in this Podunk college town…"

"What? No!" answered the man, offended. "I d-don't do that sort of thing!"

"What kind of thing would that be?" Trent pressed, taking a single step back, allowing his captive a chance to breathe. "The fuck buddy thing, or the male on male thing?"

The line of conversation was obviously having some effect. Trent enjoyed seeing the torment in the man's chiseled face as those features squirmed beneath a short crop of brown hair. The more he did it, the cuter the little guy became.

Then came the icing on the cake.

"The… um… f-thing," the stranger replied, his cheeks flushed.

"'The f-thing?' So innocent!" Trent observed with a laugh. There was something about this one; he liked the prospect and wanted more. "By the looks of you, I would have thought you liked that sort of thing."

"W-what? What's that supposed to mean?" he asked sheepishly. "Me? N-no..."

Trent nodded confidently, the man shaking his head at the same time with equal fervor.

"Okay fine, you don't have to answer that. But," Trent said, raising a fist and casually cracking his knuckles, "you still haven't told me *who* you are."

"Jonny," the man replied right away. "J-Jonny Cameron."

"Nice to *finally* meet you, Jonny," Trent replied, slapping him on the shoulder. "Seriously, any friend of Jared's is a friend of mine. The name's Trent; I own the place. Our mutual buddy Jared rents one of the bedrooms upstairs from me. So, have you been hiding out in there all day?"

Jonny went from relieved to looking positively terrified again. He didn't know how to take Trent, all bulging and intimating.

"I wasn't *hiding* up there," he retorted. "I had a long bus ride in today, so decided to take a nap while Jared went out to see..."

"Relax, Jonny," Trent said, at last moving away while flashing a rather friendly smile. "I don't need all the nitty-gritty details; this isn't an interrogation. I get it. So, I gather you're here to visit for the whole week?"

Jonny felt an immense weight lift off his shoulders. His breathing slowed, although he wasn't sure if it Trent's words caused it, or the perfect teeth they flowed past.

"Yes," Jonny told him. "Jared asked me to come out here since we both didn't have class for the week. He has a lot of things planned apparently."

"Those can be fun," Trent said, "but aren't my thing anymore."

"I can tell," Jonny said, casting his eyes over Trent's shirtless body; they loitered for a second, and he let out a half-sigh, half-moan. "The gym is your thing, I bet. I'd love to have a body like that."

Trent tensed like a reflex, his muscles tight.

"You can have it."

"Huh?" Jonny hesitated, partially hoping Trent was making an offer.

"A body like this," Trent clarified. "You can have one."

Jonny came back to reality.

"Oh, well, I've tried before without much success."

"Why's that?" Trent asked.

"One: look at me. I'm a little runt. Two: classes," Jonny said, "not to mention studies, side jobs, dieting…"

"Sounds like a list of excuses to me," Trent stated nonchalantly. "It's easier to say why you can't do something opposed to just making the time and getting it done."

Jonny's eyes drifted to the wet floor.

"But, if you *really* want it," Trent said, "I'd be glad to give you some help."

Jonny perked back up.

"Yeah, I'd like that," he said.

"I certainly don't want to get in the way of you, Jared and your plans. After all, you two would make a cute couple for all those event appearances," Trent observed.

Jonny let out a chuckle, apparently having thought about that before.

"Um, no," he replied despite himself. "Jared's just a really good friend. There's nothing between us whatsoever."

"If you say so," Trent replied, not believing him. "That makes things easier for me."

"What things, exactly?" Jonny asked.

"You'll see," Trent answered, taking the time to point down to the floor. Jonny had no choice but to pass his eyes over Trent's tight underwear as he looked down too. "First, we need to get this mess cleaned up."

The two of them stepped over to the paper towels, Trent tearing off several sheets before handing Jonny the large bunch.

"Sorry about all the noise earlier," Jonny said as he grabbed them, his fingers touching Trent's rough knuckles. "I'm clumsy at times."

"Well, I hope you're not *too* clumsy," Trent replied as they both kneeled and began soaking up the water. "I can't have you messing up both my places. Now, you can apologize to me later if you're still able to talk after one of my workouts."

JONNY DIDN'T SAY ANYTHING AS he wiped the paper towels over the spilled water, thinking that he had must have misheard Trent. The silence continued until they had cleaned up the mess.

Both places? Workout? he thought while staring down at his arms; in his mind, they were puny just like the rest of him. Briefly glancing over to Trent's, he sighed. Those were thick and defined even as they gently guided the paper towels across the floor. *What did he mean by that? I'm obviously not a gym rat, and it's way early…*

Trent stood up and stretched, having soaked up the last of the splattered water. His muscles were rippling like some meaty tide.

Jonny was watching and got up a moment later after his chub subsided. He walked over to the garbage can to dump his wet towels.

"Hold that open, will you?" Trent asked with a devilish smirk on his face. He looked Jonny right in the eyes as he said, "I just have to drop my wads."

Jonny choked, more at the predator-like stare than the bad joke.

This guy is crazy, he thought, all the while finding himself liking the strange attention he was receiving.

"So, I have to ask: what did you mean earlier about working out? You can tell that I don't."

"I know," Trent said, "but I thought that's what we agreed to change."

Jonny furrowed his brow, deep lines forming across it.

"Well we did, but, I…uh, just came down for some water tonight," he said, reaching for an excuse. It wasn't going to work.

"Yeah, yeah, water is good for staying hydrated. You also said you'd like some workout tips, right? No better way to give advice than to *show* you," Trent stated, arching a brow back at him. "We decided no more excuses, or do I have to bust out the fists again?"

Jonny couldn't deny what he'd said, since as it was no more than ten minutes beforehand, but he was longing for his mattress, not a barbell.

"Right…" he replied, but far less enthusiastically than before. "I did say that but…"

Trent stepped up close to Jonny one more time.

Jonny struggled to look up, but the bigger man was quick to grab his smooth chin and guide his gaze to his.

"Listen," Trent said in a whisper; his face was unyielding. "I am not going to force you to do anything you don't want to. You're free to head right back up to your room and forget this entire conversation ever happened. Or, you can realize this is all about leaving your cushy comfort zone of excuses. In all aspects. Sometimes you have to be inconvenienced to grow. Plus, there are other benefits you're going to have working with me… ones that aren't going to be there if you leave now. I *do* want to help you, Jonny-boy; don't make me change my mind."

Jonny struggled for a moment, the smallest part of him still looking for a way out and back into his bed for sleep, but seeing the way Trent was eyeing him, the majority buckled.

"Okay," he said. "Let's do this; I know nothing so I'm at your mercy. Should we leave Jared a note or something? Let him know where we are?"

"No," Trent replied with a simple smile, stepping away toward cupboards. "He knows me well enough."

TRENT TOOK A FEW MINUTES to rummage through the cabinets. They were full of mismatched plastic cups of all sizes and colors, shaker inserts, and lids. Eventually, he reemerged, managing to match up a complete set for two small shaker cups.

"Can you grab some pre-workout?" Trent asked as he used his elbows to close the doors, stepping up to the counter beside the sink. "It'll be in that cabinet on your left, the short white container in the front."

Jonny wondered what they were mixing up, quickly opening the doors. He was greeted with a huge stack of supplements – from protein powders and pre-workouts all the way to diuretics and branched chain amino acids. It was intimidating as hell, but he did as he was told and grabbed the stubby white container with a blue label.

"Is this it?" he asked, giving it a gentle shake.

"Boom," Trent replied, twitching his neck to invite Jonny over. "Yes, it is! That should wake your ass up."

Jonny enthusiastically made his way back to Trent, holding out the tub.

Trent waved his hand, asking him to take off the lid as he finished putting the cups together.

Jonny nodded in reply, but as he tried the lid hardly budged.

"My bad," Trent apologized, noticing the struggle and Jonny's frown, "I guess I must've been in a mood last night and tightened that a bit too much. Here, let me…"

Jonny wasn't about to let some lid deflate him and was still trying to get it off as Trent talked. Finally, the lid wrestled free, but the rest of the container went tumbling to the floor. It bounced a couple of times with a chastising *thud*, coming to rest gingerly at Trent's feet.

Powder was everywhere, even on the back of Trent's form fitting undies that clung to his round ass.

"Way to go," Trent said sarcastically, twisting his narrow waist to look at Jonny. His eyes were seductively slim. "That was *only* forty bucks."

"Crap," Jonny said while cowering, "I am so sorry."

Something about this guy turned Trent on as he saw him worrying. He wasn't another muscled-up iron-head; as enjoyable as that was, it was getting stale. Perhaps it was entirely because he wasn't one – the polar opposite of what Trent looked at in the mirror daily. Whatever the reason, Trent could feel urges mounting and he wanted them to overflow.

"Don't worry, you'll be paying for it somehow," Trent continued.

He wasn't mad at all, instead swiping his hand across the back side of his underwear. His fingers picked up some of the chalky residue. When he brought his hand back around, he slapped it hard against his dick, which swung heavily beneath the fabric.

"Well," Trent said cockily as his eyes bounced from Jonny's astonished gaze straight down his rippled front, "are you going to clean this shit up or not?"

Another smirk had formed on Trent's face, and if Jonny didn't know better, a bulge was rising to the south in his pants.

"Y-yeah, sure," Jonny said nervously, yet his body responded without a hint of delay. Before he knew what he was doing, Jonny was down on the floor, kneeling in front of Trent's large thighs. Being so close only served to underscore the differences in their size and definition. Trent's legs were like tree trunks compared to Jonny's sticks, but that didn't matter right now.

Using his hands to brush off the loose powder, Jonny watched as Trent flexed his muscled legs, their veins and lines rising and falling out of view. He also felt something thrilling beneath the cotton and with each pass of his hand, it grew even more so.

Trent was also paying close attention, looking down the ridges of his eight-pack as Jonny cleaned up the mess he caused. He could tell that Jonny was tempted to nuzzle his face against his building erection, watching as the young man brought the fabric ever so close to his nostrils with each pass. Trent rewarded him with a thrust forward, and as soon as the material met his skin, Jonny greedily took in Trent's scent. Letting out a subtle growl, like a beast in a cage that was about to be set free, Trent could tell that his cock easily rivaled the little guy's wrist for thickness and it all nearly sent him rocketing to full size.

Jonny responded with lightning speed, latching onto Trent's underwear band. He wanted to yank them down and tried to do so but was stopped by Trent's formidable grip.

Trent pulled Jonny straight up onto his feet with very little effort, dipping his head down to meet him.

"Not so innocent after all, I see. Almost made me break a rule," Trent murmured sternly into Jonny's ear, the warm air tickling as it passed. "Not here, ever. Plus, we still have work to do. No excuses for you, remember?"

Jonny, breathing heavily, was still relishing the view and smells circling him. He found a new like for the area around Trent's chest and neck, burying his face in that space.

"Okay," he said reluctantly, not wanting to move. "We better head out."

CHAPTER 2

THE RIDE

ABOUT FIFTEEN MINUTES HAD PASSED since the two left Trent's hillside home, the darkness around the '69 Charger profound and foreboding, yet Jonny wasn't nervous – even though he was in a car at nearly four in the morning with someone he'd met less than an hour before.

Stop thinking about it and enjoy yourself, he told himself. *The guy knows Jared, so you're in good hands.*

Yeah, said another voice, *hands attached to muscles that can wring your little neck if you're not more careful, dumbass.*

Jonny liked the former voice much better, choosing to focus on it versus the one championing potential murder by muscle-man, as hot as that might be. In fact, looking at Trent's concentrated face as he drove them into town, he oddly found some solace in its rugged features and a level of protection he hadn't had since he'd left home – and his ex – for college. It was strange to be thinking that way, and Jonny wondered if it was caused by the pre-workout they had taken.

Jonny had changed into a clean pair of gym shorts that Trent had plucked from his closet, along with the smallest tank top he had. Apparently, it was one an old client had forgotten after his last training session and somehow, it found a home amongst some of the big man's favorite tanks. Jonny thought that he looked silly in the outfit because it was slightly oversized; he felt like it wasn't him at all.

The car continued down the road, jostling the two of them with dips and the odd pothole that couldn't be avoided.

"Our government and tax dollars at work," Trent snapped, looking briefly at his young passenger. He reached out and set a large hand on Jonny's slim thigh as if to steady him.

Jonny made a fist and bumped it twice against the back of Trent's hand, scared to let any feelings lead him to grabbing hold of it. However, after getting worked up with fretful thinking, something told him to stop and he went ahead and set his hand on top of Trent's.

"Your hesitation's okay," Trent said. "I'm not known as a romantic guy. Hate the shit actually."

"I can tell," Jonny added with a nervous laugh, catching an approving side glance from Trent. "That's fine with me, though. I'm not looking for that sort of thing these days. At least, not right now."

"Past issues?" Trent asked, flipping the turn signal on before changing lanes and making a left turn.

"You could say that," Jonny added. "The ex, living back in Marshall, took a lot of pleasure in putting me down, all the while using me as a stepping stone to pick himself up."

"Oh, how I can relate to that," Trent agreed, moving his hand along Jonny's leg. "Motherfuckers."

"In a way, you remind me of him," Jonny added right as Trent spoke. He expected Trent to flip out yet he didn't, but Jonny apologized regardless.

"No need for that," Trent said. "I'm *easily* that kind of guy if you didn't already notice – carefree and used to getting what I want. A lot see that sort of thing as arrogance or pride, wanting everyone else to fit in nice little baskets in front of nice bikes taking the high roads. Fuck that. I see myself as being different, successful, and true to myself. And I like it. None of us have time for fake, so for me the equation's simple: be real or get out of my way."

Jonny nodded.

"Hell, look at tonight," Trent continued. "I wanted you, and here you are, in the car like clockwork."

"Hey!" Jonny huffed, his features scrunched.

"Just returning the comparison," Trent said with a little laugh. "I didn't mean it, much."

"Touché," Jonny responded. "That's one thing I struggle with and need to learn: how to be true to myself."

"Yes, you do," Trent said. "This little trip is one step. But enough of that; we're getting a little too personal."

"Before we shift and talk about weights and shakes, you're not one to get close to people, are you?"

"No," Trent stated. "I'm not a romantic and I don't usually like to kiss either. It forms too much of an emotional bond and, well, baggage."

"*Usually?*" Jonny pressed.

Trent just grunted.

"Hey, how old are you anyway?" he asked as retail buildings started to appear on both sides of the road.

"Twenty-one," Jonny replied. "Well, twenty-two in a week and a half. You?"

"Twenty-five."

"Why'd you ask?"

"No particular reason," Trent answered. "Honestly just forgot earlier. I like to know my client's details, so I have my bearings when working with them."

"More like stats than details, eh? Are the bearings for *your* fuck buddy clients or your personal training clients?" Jonny asked, wearing a shit-eating grin.

Trent mumbled something indecipherable under his breath, though Jonny got the message when Trent squeezed the hand still resting on his leg, hard.

AFTER A FEW MORE BUMPY turns, the duo pulled up into the empty parking lot of the Summerset Center, a collection of shops on the north part of Logan. Ahead of them was an assortment of darkened storefronts, the only light streaming into the vehicle from a collection of large, block letters hanging between a frozen yogurt spot and a clothes store.

"Swole," said Jonny, bathed in the sign's red light. "Odd name for a gym. Is that where we're headed?"

"Bingo," replied Trent, switching the engine off and reaching into the back seat for his gym bag. "It's a cool name, too. I mean, that's why a lot of people go there, isn't it?"

"I wouldn't really know. Plus, it looks closed," Jonny noticed, squinting as he tried to look inside the windows. "None of the lights are on."

"We'll be fine," Trent replied, producing a set of keys from the bag. "Welcome to my home away from home."

The car doors opened and both men stepped out into the slightly chilly air.

"So, you own the place?" asked Jonny as they walked up to the front. He had a much better view of the inside and though it was still dark, he found all the equipment intimidating.

"Yes sir," Trent replied, jangling his keys until the front door popped open. He swung it and entered, quickly keying in a code on a panel to the side.

Jonny walked in after him, the air markedly warmer inside.

"Hey, can you hit that switch right there, to your right?" Trent asked as he tossed the keys back in his bag, adjusting it across his broad shoulder. It strained against the tight baseball shirt he had on.

Jonny hit the switch and the lights flickered, filling the room a few seconds later. The gym was laid out ahead of him, an overwhelming playground of cardio equipment, free weights, plates, and machines.

"It's bigger than I expected," Jonny said as he stepped forward.

"That's what they all say," Trent replied.

Jonny rolled his eyes.

"Follow me," Trent indicated with a head tilt. "This way to the locker room. I have to change real quick."

As they walked through the iron jungle, Trent gave Jonny a brief tour of the place. The newbie had already taken stock of the equipment, but was made aware of the different rooms that had been set up for different body parts. There was another for just for cycling and even a movie theater to pass the time on treadmills. Jonny had no idea that gyms could be so elaborate.

"Fun eh?" Trent said confidently, his eyes lingering on the squat rack in a side room as they passed.

Dammit I wish it was leg day... he thought, his gaze then drifting over to a flat bench press in the next room. A smirk formed on his face as he looked casually over his shoulder to Jonny, who had fallen behind to look at some poster sized prints of Trent that were hanging on the wall.

"Those photos were from last year. God, time flies. I did a local competition and placed pretty well," Trent told him. "From there I could have gone for nationals, but opening this place took priority. I may try again next year. I *did* shoot with a pretty cool photographer at the time; he had come up from the south. Since then we've become good friends. Those are some of the favorite ones he took of me."

"That's a lot of hard work, man," Jonny said, impressed by what he was looking at.

"Thanks!" Trent replied. "Like I told you, anything is possible if you make the time for it. It doesn't happen overnight, though."

"Yeah, for real," Jonny said as he stood there, still amazed by the physique in the pictures. It was even more defined than the person with him now. The thought of running his hands all over made him...

"Hey! Jonny-boy!" Trent's voice cut through his fantasy. "Let's move! I'm going to need your help, and we have about an hour and a half before the place opens up."

Jonny snapped to attention and scurried the rest of the way to the locker room, wondering what the hell Trent would need help with. His body lingered in his mind the entire way.

Trent was already at a locker when Jonny walked in. The walls were gray and the lockers themselves a dark blue. Wooden benches were set along the middle, leading to a shower area and what looked like a sauna beyond.

Jonny tried not to stare, but his eyes fell on something hypnotic. He watched as Trent stepped out of his shorts and removed his underwear, giving Jonny his first unobstructed view of the manhood he toyed with earlier. His asshole puckered at the sight. Although he was soft, Trent's thick dick swung around, probably bigger than a lot of guys were hard.

He gulped as Trent noticed, turning to show off his bare ass. It was sculpted from years of working out and his trunk like legs did nothing to make it any less spectacular.

"No restrictions here like back at the house," Trent told him as he removed a pair of sweat shorts from the locker. Stepping into each leg, he bent over – nearly causing Jonny to faint – while slowly shifting and pulling until they were fully raised.

The sweats were sticking snugly around him, and when he turned back around the large visible penis line was unmistakable, hardly contained in the shorts.

"So, once you get your jaw off the floor, I'm going to need your help," Trent said.

Jonny's thoughts were a bit incoherent, but he still managed to approach his new trainer without stumbling over his own feet.

"I just need you to help me get this shirt off," Trent stated. "It's new, and I don't want to stretch it out the first time wearing it."

Jonny passed his eyes over the shirt. It was white in the middle with three-quarter sleeves that were bright red. There was a centerpiece with a large black skull grenade. All of it was very tight, showing off the width of Trent's back and shoulders.

"I just noticed the design on the shirt," Jonny said.

"Kickass design, right?" Trent said enthusiastically. "Another one of my buddies out in Missouri started up the line. Love the skulls."

"Yeah, they're really cool," Jonny said as he grabbed the bottom of the shirt.

Trent stepped closer, raising his arms up high. His natural scent, mixed with beard balm, filled his nostrils as Jonny pulled the shirt up, slowly revealing a pair of deep v-lines that plunged into Trent's sweats. Above them were eight distinct ridges on his torso. Jonny continued to lift higher, Trent turning around when Jonny reached his chest.

"This is the tough part, they always catch on my lats," Trent said, flaring his back as if he was on the competition stage.

"Well, have you ever thought about getting a bigger shirt?" Jonny asked as he hooked his fingers under the straining fabric.

"Yeah," Trent replied, shifting his weight so that his perfect ass was sticking out along with the sexy lines of his lower back, "Once the next size looks just as tight as this one on me."

Jonny snickered, inching the body-hugging shirt up and around Trent's width. He was so close that he could lick the back of Trent's neck with little effort. The thick muscles were too enticing to ignore.

No restrictions here? Jonny thought, going ahead and licking Trent right then and there.

Trent sighed and backed his ass up to Jonny's crotch at the same time, finding his dick had started to tent his shorts.

"Damn, I'm impressed," Trent said as he ground his ass against Jonny once before stepping forward again. "Maybe later this week, Jonny-boy."

Jonny found himself getting even harder, his cock already finding a way out of the confines of his underwear, seeking a means out of his shorts. He continued to take the shirt off, growing larger the higher it went. At last, he passed the widest point, managing to roll the shirt completely off and Trent was shirtless again in front of him. Jonny was impressed, inspired, and intoxicated by what he saw.

Trent didn't leave much time for additional thoughts, spinning around to grab a black square-cut tank top from the locker. He slid it over himself while Jonny watched the fabric lock away his fantasy, for the time being at least.

"You sure do know how to motivate a man," Jonny whispered.

"That I do," Trent replied, reaching around to grab hold of Jonny's ass. "Do well and I'll give you some more motivation. Now, let's get you educated on how to build up your chest."

CHAPTER 3

THE WORKOUT

TRENT LED THE WAY FROM the locker rooms into the second room to the right. The floor was covered in a spongy, black mat and along the far was a full set of heavy free weights that ranged from five all the way to one-hundred-fifty pounds.

"I guess we'll be on that end," Jonny said, pointing toward the fives.

"Depends on where you're currently at," Trent said, walking past forty-five-pound weight plates hanging behind a trio of workout benches:

one flat, one inclined, one declined. "We'll be using those tonight, but also these here. Maybe the cables over there if you're up for it too."

"It's been a while, so I have no idea where I'm at," said Jonny nervously, picking up the fives and finding them very light. "But, given how these feel I guess I can move up a little."

"Good," Trent said with a tiny smile, telling him about the general routine they were going to go through. It was geared toward beginners and gaining mass, but it worked.

"We're going to be doing all that in an hour?" Jonny said, already tired from listening to it.

"Yes, I keep a quick pace," Trent said pointedly. "So don't be a whiny bitch."

"I'm…" Jonny began but was quickly silenced by Trent's dominate stare.

"Trust me I won't let you break or tear anything. This isn't about ego; it's about results."

That was reassuring, but something told Jonny that Trent did more ego-lifting than he led on.

They kicked off doing some dumbbell flyes to warm up, Trent grabbing a pair of forty-fives while Jonny tried the twenty-fives.

"Wider," Trent directed as he watched Jonny perform the movement, "and be sure to squeeze at the top."

Jonny was struggling to keep good form while wanting to use weights that didn't make him look weak. Especially in front of Trent.

"Here," Trent said, handing him some that were ten pounds lighter. "Use these and watch your form. If you do it wrong, you aren't maximizing your workout, but you *are* increasing the chance of injury. I told you that I'm going to make sure that doesn't happen."

He leaned down close to Jonny's ear as he positioned the weights.

"At least out here…"

Jonny was motivated and performed his second set of ten repetitions with a determined grin on his face. Trent guided him, keeping his elbows in the proper position with his rugged hands.

"That's much better," Trent said. "Can you feel the difference?

"Yeah," Jonny said. "Thanks."

THE ROUTINE CONTINUED FROM FLYES to some dumbbell presses, then the benches.

Jonny was fascinated by Trent's swelling chest, gnarly veins appearing the more they pumped and the more blood that surged into them. Looking down at his, there was a slight redness but nothing that was close to what his trainer was showing.

As they moved over to the incline bench, Trent suggested they switch up for this one before moving to the cables to finish. He wanted to knock out a couple of heavier sets while he could and then swap, letting him focus fully on Jonny's entire set.

"That works for me," Jonny agreed, helping Trent load up two-hundred-thirty pounds on the already forty-five-pound bar.

Usually this would have intimidated Jonny, watching someone bigger than him lifting a lot of weight; he would not have stuck around. There was something different about this situation, though, and Trent kept him glued in position.

Grunting and keeping great form, Trent blasted through three full sets, sweating and swollen by the end of them. His arms and chest looked like they were about to burst as they moved to take the weights off in preparation for Jonny's much lighter set. Jonny took up position and Trent climbed up on the short step to spot him.

"I like the view from here," Jonny joked as he stared right up Trent's beastly body.

Sweat made its way down his neck and over his huge chest into his tank top, where Jonny imagined each glistening bead making its way over his chiseled stomach.

"Shhh for now," Trent responded. "Just lift."

Jonny had gotten through three of his four sets, the bar settling into its holster with a *clang*. His eyes were closed and his breathing heavy, riding a high of pre-workout energy and satisfaction that he was actually getting through a real workout. Jonny could hear Trent breathing hard as well. Slowly opening his eyes, he nearly fainted at what he saw.

Trent was standing over him, his massive erection dangling out of one leg of his sweat shorts. It swung like a meaty pendulum above him, a long strand of pre-cum hypnotizing as it flirted with him; growing longer and getting closer.

Trent helped things along, squatting slightly while pressing his arms and chest against the bar like some push up. His round chest peeked out from the top of his tank top while he brought his delicious dick closer to Jonny's needy lips.

Jonny tasted all of that wet goodness first, licking his lips as Trent's wide head danced across his quivering mouth.

"You sure about this?" Trent grunted.

Jonny didn't say a word, taking it in and causing Trent to pant. The monster broke the seal on its way toward Jonny's throat, causing his cock to strain against the confines of his briefs.

Trent willingly plunged deeper, and Jonny loved what he could see, taste, and smell. It was exhilarating even though Trent's balls were still locked away behind those shorts. It didn't bother Jonny at all; he was making sure to enjoy every inch he could accommodate.

Trent tugged on Jonny's head by his hair, allowing his dick to slip further down his warm, tight throat. He loved seeing lips stretched to capacity by his shaft, moving his fingers around Jonny's ears for more leverage as he bottomed out. He pulled back quickly, giving Jonny a fleeting chance for breath, only to ram it mercilessly forward again and again.

Jonny was spread to his max but continued to let Trent go to town, even though he was grappling to breathe through his aching throat and skirted gagging more than a couple of times. Seeing the underside of that massive cock as he was getting skull-fucked to oblivion was well worth every twinge and cramp he could feel. And boy could he feel everything as Trent's rhythm became erratic and his dick began to throb with a mind of its own.

He was about to pass the point of no return.

Jonny didn't know if he could handle it, nearly reaching orgasm himself...

Right before Trent blew his load, there was a sound outside. It was the front door opening then closing again.

Jonny slid down, Trent falling out of his mouth. Jerking away, he had a look of shock on his face.

"What the hell was that?" Jonny asked between gasps. "I thought you said the place wasn't open until five-thirty?"

"It's not," Trent replied, unfazed. His dick was still hard as a rock. "It's just Lisa, the cleaner. She's here to do her rounds."

"What the fuck?" Jonny exclaimed, bolting up from the bench and swiping his hands through his hair. His erection had long gone into hiding. "Oh gosh, what if she catches us?"

Trent looked unbothered, giving himself a couple of strokes that teased out an enormous amount of pre-cum. He dabbled in it with his fingers before wiping it all over his rod.

"She knows me, too," he said indifferently. "Besides, she won't be back here for another fifteen or twenty minutes."

Jonny's heart was beating nervously.

"I... uh... can't..." Jonny stuttered. "I can't do this."

"It's all good man," Trent said, stuffing his meat back into the shorts. "I get it. Let's wrap this workout up then and hit the showers. I'm sure Jared has a lot of things planned with you for the day, and I'll have clients coming in tomorrow that I need to prep for."

"Okay," said Jonny relieved, if not a little exhilarated by the experience he just had. He looked over to Trent as he was setting up the cables for their last routine and a depressing thought hit him hard in the gut.

Jonny, what if you just ruined any more chances of training with benefits?

"Come on Jonny," Trent said firmly, confirming the joy ride was over. "We have work to finish."

"Coming," Jonny replied, kicking himself inside as he reached the cables.

THE TWO OF THEM CONTINUED with their last exercises on the cable machine, using them for flyes in the high, middle, and lower positions one right after another.

By the third set Jonny's chest was on fire, and he suspected Trent had picked up the pace and threw in these supersets not only to punish him physically, but also to get the routine over and done quickly. There was no light banter between the two of them since starting, just a wall of pure professionalism.

Off in the distance, Lisa had started a vacuum cleaner, its loud hum reaching the duo as they began their final set. Despite its annoying drone, it seemed to narrow the divide.

"I'm impressed that you've managed to keep up the pace this morning, Jonny," said Trent as he observed from behind. "Less leaning forward and be sure to keep your feet apart for stability. It'll keep your core tighter, too.

"Okay," Jonny replied. The pre-workout must have been wearing off because these last flyes were pure torture. "You know what Trent? Despite my appearances, I've always been a bit of a competitive guy. Mainly in school though, not this physical jock stuff."

"You've done well," Trent said. "Definitely not a raw beginner. I bet that I can outlast you the rest of the week, though. Want to wager?"

Jonny was beaming on the inside; Trent still wanted to see him.

"That depends on what the bet is," Jonny replied. "Given the penalty, I just might lose."

Trent chuckled as he stepped over to drop one side of the cable machine all the way to the floor.

"Mind getting the other side too?" Jonny asked, taking the opportunity to admire the curves that were facing him.

Trent didn't say a word as he stood back upright, swaggering over to the other side where he lowered that assembly too.

"Thank you," Jonny said innocently, pulling on the cables up to begin.

Trent grunted and kept watching.

"Good form this time; I like what I'm seeing."

Jonny lifted his gaze to the mirror as he squeezed the rep tightly.

"Lucky you," he said, "because all I can see is one big prick behind me."

Trent put his hands on his hips, and somehow his dick seemed to protrude more.

"Oh really?" Trent asked. "Well, I know of another one you'll be having a close chat with soon enough."

The last three reps were a breeze for Jonny, having found a second wind and a growing mast to sail. Squeezing long and hard a final time, he let go of the cables and the plates clashed against each other loudly.

"All done," said Trent, approaching from the back.

He dipped his thumbs into each side of Jonny's shorts, swooping them around the top until they met at the center of his back. He then tugged the shorts away from his body, glancing down at the prize. There was a thin line of sweat drizzled down the middle of Jonny's expectant ass.

"I like what I see there," Trent said as he reached in to spread the wetness around with a thumb.

Jonny tensed up as he rubbed, Trent letting out a little laugh as he watched Jonny's cheeks tighten.

"What's the matter?" Trent asked. "Seems like your hole is trying to pass itself off as innocent like you tried earlier?"

Jonny turned, looking over his shoulder.

"F-stuff," Trent said.

"Why don't you put all that money where your dirty mouth is, big boy?" Jonny replied.

"Okay then," Trent said with a quick slap on the ass. "It's time I delivered on my end of the bargain."

CHAPTER 4

ULTRAVIOLET

TRENT, NEARLY RUPTURING HIS TOO-SMALL tank top from all angles, had a hand clasped firmly around the ties at the front of Jonny's athletic shorts, guiding him like a dog on a leash toward the locker room.

Jonny found himself giddy if not a little lightheaded as he trailed behind, looking around from side to side one more time. Before they reached their destination, Jonny happened to glance off to this right. There was a narrowly open door, beyond which something that looked like a standing tanning booth.

"Hey Trent," Jonny called. "What's in there?"

Trent looked off to the right and muttered under his breath.

"I told them to keep that locked during off-hours," he said with irritation in his voice. "It's one of our three tanning booths. Apparently, the staff doesn't listen very well and left that one unlocked overnight."

"You should tell the owner of this place," Jonny replied, "after we use it, of course. Unless you're worried about getting into trouble…"

Trent stopped in dead his tracks and gave Jonny a look that was like kindling for a fire. Jonny's dick had no choice but to start getting hard.

"I'll tell him alright," Trent said. "Though according to you he's a big prick."

"You misheard me then," Jonny stated. "I said he *has* a big prick and as it so happens, I earned some time with it."

"You want it in there?" Trent said, nodding toward the tanning booth.

"In *me*," Jonny said, wasting no time walking into the small room, this time leading Trent.

Entering the area, Jonny noticed how small the room was. There was a large cylindrical tanning both – new and shiny and upright – along with a small bench to change clothes and a full-length mirror. In it, he spotted Trent coming in and closing the door. He locked it right after.

"There, now you shouldn't be worried about Lisa interrupting us," Trent said. "I'm sure the thought of a woman coming in here and seeing us going hard at it is off-putting to you."

"That just proves that you don't know me very well," said Jonny. "Yet."

Trent grinned; he hadn't come across someone like this before. Normally the huge guys he dominated with his dick were slow, methodical, and predictable. In other words, a complete yawn-fest.

Jonny was something new and fresh, and Trent made a decision right there that he had never done before. He was going to see this guy for the entire week. Who the fuck knew where things would end up, but it was already a hundred times better than his last ten encounters.

"Looking forward to that then," Trent said as he pried apart the tanning booth doors.

The inside looked like a futuristic escape pod, the bottom of the unit like a bouncy trampoline. Vertical lamps surrounded the interior, including the doors, and above a set of handles was a control box.

"Take off your clothes," Trent ordered, stepping back to watch as Jonny complied.

Off came the tank top first, cast casually to the floor. Jonny's short and slender frame held onto the small pump from the previous workout and even though he had a long way to go to match Trent, he was fucking fantastic to look at in his own right. Then, the shorts slipped off and were on the ground, Jonny's small yet perky ass screaming to be touched, licked, and fucked. Then he turned around, and Trent's dick surged with blood. The little guy was not as little as he thought from the front. In fact, Jonny was damn near as large as Trent was, albeit thinner.

Jonny stepped inside the booth, discovering that the floor was firm, and he moved forward to play with the handles while Trent undressed behind him.

A few seconds later, Jonny felt the embrace of vast arms around him, Trent's hard chest and abs pressing against Jonny's back as he arched backward. Trent encased Jonny's body, dropping his head down to spur Jonny's quaking along with a few nuzzles of beard hair against the young man's neck.

Trent then turned him around and their eyes met, Jonny biting one of his lips as his heart rate rose. He tried to look away, but it was useless. Trent's eyes were so intense and green, Jonny became trapped in those emerald jewels.

It was surreal being in this position with anyone to begin with, but being with someone as good looking and fit like Trent blew Jonny's mind.

The heat was already rising in the room and the booth was not even on. Jonny felt it spreading around his body so quickly that he wanted to faint while Trent, so stoic, remained still, keenly watching Jonny's every move.

It's when Trent saw Jonny's throat move as he gulped that he rushed forward, his wanting lips crashing into Jonny's with such an intense fire the world around them could burn to cinders. They stood there, naked and together, kissing so passionately and embracing one another so tightly it was a miracle they could breathe.

Jonny moaned as their bodies churned against each other, the salty-sweet aromas whipping them into a sexually charged frenzy that caused their dicks to drool all over the place.

Trent seized the base of Jonny's cock, stroking it slowly to tease it to full size. It wasn't small in the slightest, and since the end was slick with excitement, there was ample lube for the rest of his long shaft as Trent worked it hard.

Jonny did the same, grabbing hold of Trent's large balls first before looking down in amazement when his hand couldn't close entirely around Trent's girth. Nevertheless, he fondled his trainer's raging hard-on like he'd never done with anyone before. With each pass along those nine inches, Jonny realized that Trent had him beat, and since he lost, he would have to pay the price.

Bring it on, he thought.

Feeling the excitement, Trent grew into a beast, flipping Jonny back around and making sure he had his arms up on the handles. A hand glided around Jonny's throat, delicately massaging it while Trent's thick beard bristled against the back of Jonny's neck, the wetness of Trent's lips smattering the area in tender kisses.

"Push that green button," Trent said as he licked Jonny, going down his neck along the full length of his back.

Jonny did and the room became a swirl of rushing air, blue lights, and incredible heat.

Trent had paused at the top of Jonny's ass, savoring the blue-hued view for a moment before spreading his cheeks apart and burying himself, beard and all inside.

"Whoa, hey…" Jonny started before he gasped and his eyes fluttered, the combination of Trent's beard alongside the broad lashes from his wet tongue was heavenly. He groaned as Trent lapped at him, teasing Jonny's hole into anticipatory spasms. It wasn't long before sweat started to pour off their bodies.

Trent stood back upright, seemingly done.

"Full of promises aren't…" Jonny began to complain, stopping as soon as he felt a single slick finger where Trent had been feasting, swirling around.

"Oh really now?" said Trent, generously adding a second finger to slip around.

Jonny moaned lightly as he felt the first finger breach him, his hole devouring it.

"More," he begged.

Trent didn't delay, sending another thick finger inside, seeking out Jonny's pleasure point. It wasn't long before the pair of fingers found it, causing the little guy to heave with gratification. Trent tortured him for a while, slowly dragging his dense fingers in and out of Jonny's tight hole.

"There's no mistaking that they found it," Trent grunted, going ahead and sending in all four fingers to massage Jonny inside.

Jonny snapped his eyes shut, unable to open them; the rush of sensations was too much. Instead, he let out a guttural moan that caused Trent to gush pre-cum down his leg.

Jonny gripped the handles with all his strength as Trent continued massaging him, staving a collapse to the floor in agonizing bliss.

"Want me to stop?" Trent asked, his tone indicating he had no intentions of doing so.

"No..." Jonny whimpered.

"No what?"

"No, sir... don't fucking stop."

Trent's fingers continued and Jonny bellowed, waves of ecstasy rushed throughout his body. His dick hardened, driving him close to the point of unconsciousness.

"I'm not done yet," Trent promised, pulling his fingers out only to be joined by his thumb.

O-oh m-my G-god! Jonny thought, even his mind stuttering. He was not only amazed that he could accommodate this, but that it felt so amazingly good.

Jonny used one of his hands to start stroking his cock while the other was still latched firmly onto a handle for support. He worked his long shaft while Trent dug away at him, the overbearing sensations reaching fever pitch.

"Okay, Jonny-boy," Trent said after a few minutes of action. "That's all you get of *that* for now."

He pulled out and Jonny's asshole snapped closed, twitching with regret.

That's when Trent laid a hand on Jonny's waist, guiding the tip of his shaft against his hole with the other. Once he pushed the head inside – causing Jonny to shudder – he too grabbed the handles and began to tear Jonny a new asshole, each stroke hard and more unforgiving than the last.

Jonny's forehead struck the walls of the booth, but he didn't care, the pleasurable aching in his ass sweeping that temporary pain away. He took hold of his cock again and pumped away in unison with every one of Trent's thrusts.

God, it felt so good, so right that he didn't want it to end.

By the slowing of Trent's changing rhythm, he didn't want it to end either.

They were both getting close, the heat of the tanning booth blending with the heat of their bodies which became inseparable and as one. Jonny could feel Trent building toward an orgasm, his thickening dick throbbing with pressure. That alone sent Jonny toppling over the edge. His legs bent beneath him as his cock exploded in neon glory, scattering cum in every direction. Eight thick ropes splashed against the walls, lamps, and floor.

Trent let go of the handles, tracing bowed fingers like claws down Jonny's back, leaving red lines in his wake. His grunts were low, and his thrusting picked up speed again until he was flung over the edge and powerless to stop. He came while burrowed deep inside Jonny, overflowing as his balls roiled in the slippery mix. After a final, prolonged grind, he withdrew and set himself atop Jonny's equally spent frame where they rested until the booth turned off.

Kicking the door open behind him, Trent let the normal light of the room fill the small chamber.

Jonny stirred, at last, turning to face Trent. Even though they were both a mess inside and out, Jonny latched hold of Trent tightly, not wanting to let go.

"What's this?" Trent said with a tone of surprise. "I told you I didn't get involved in romantic junk like this."

Jonny wiped one of his hands through Trent's hair before stroking his beard.

"You also told me you don't kiss either," Jonny retorted. "I seem to recall plenty of that sort of thing, but I could be mistaken – since I was nearly out of my mind at a couple of points."

"I said *usually*," Trent clarified.

Jonny nodded.

"Ah, I see," he stated. "So, it's safe to say that I'm not one of your regular fuck buddies then?"

Trent eyed the little guy whose eyes were just higher than his chest.

"What the hell have you gone and done to me, Jonny-boy?" Trent asked, uncaring of what the answer was. He leaned down to snatch another long kiss before Jonny could reply.

Hesitantly, the two separated, ready for a shower but unwilling to get on with their days.

"See you tonight?" asked Jonny with a big smile.

Trent smirked as he bobbed his head, making his way out of the booth.

"Unless Jared throws you something better than I did, of course. I know for a fact it's not going to be bigger."

"Jared who?" Jonny replied casually and they both laughed.

"Do have a good time with him today, okay?" Trent urged as he wiped his dick off with his tank top, tossing it to Jonny to wipe up. "I wouldn't have had the chance to nearly beat the shit out of you if he hadn't invited you up."

"Glad you didn't, though you roughed me up in other ways," Jonny said. "Super happy about that."

Trent chuckled at his talents.

"I do have one more question, though," Jonny said in a rough, beaten whisper.

Trent eyed him cautiously as he put on his snug shorts. "What are we working out next?"

THE END

SWOLE: LEG DAY

Published and written by: Golden Czermak
2nd Edition

ACKNOWLEDGEMENTS

This work would not be possible without such great support from readers and others in the book community.

Special thanks to all my tree-trunk legged gym bros for inspiring this part of the erotic short story series. Squats for the win. #ThirdLeg

SWOLE
LEG DAY

CHAPTER 1

AFTER CHEST DAY

THE HANDLE ON THE FRONT door of a modern, hillside home jostled. Behind it was the sound of frustrated grunts and whispers.

"One more fucking thing to replace in this joint…" said a muffled voice, the man who owned it unmistakably aggravated. There was another rattle and the low *thump* of a shoulder against the wood. "Damn latch has started sticking again; it does this every time the weather …"

He didn't get to finish the sentence, the door unexpectedly opening as it flung toward the wall. A quick and calloused hand grabbed it just before it struck. It was attached to a muscular arm that, in turn, hung out of a wrinkly sleeveless tee.

"That was close," he said, giving his thick beard a good scouring with his fingertips. Adjusting a gym bag that hung off his broad shoulder, the man swaggered into the dark foyer.

"No kidding, Trent," said a shorter, thinner silhouette as it followed, closing the unruly door behind them. "That dent would have been yet another thing for you to repair."

"Yeah, yeah Jonny-boy, point out the obvious," Trent replied, smirking as he turned to see Jonny standing there all innocent and cute. He knew that appearance was deceiving. Looking up to the ceiling, Trent pointed and said, "I was thinking more about waking the sleeping beast that is Jared Hughes. Frankly, I don't want to deal with any of his bullshit right now."

Bullshit? Jonny wondered, his face squashed together as if he'd bitten a large chunk out of a lemon. *From Jared? What'd he mean by that?*

There was obviously some water under the bridge, but before Jonny could ask Trent was talking again.

"Besides," he continued, emerald eyes locked back on Jonny, "I don't think you'd mind seeing me work hard... *again.*"

With that said, Trent's smirk became a lip bite and he reached down to the ends of his tee, stripping it off. As the fabric rolled over the tight curves and deep lines of his upper body, they seemed to gleam with a light of their own.

Jonny's eyes widened, and his asshole twitched, thinking of the time the two spent entangled with and inside each other last night – or rather that morning – at Trent's gym. Jonny realized that it was aptly named Swole and not just for the muscles that got a good pump within its walls.

"Jesus that needs to be washed," Trent said of the shirt, casually dropping it to the floor. "Oops."

Jonny snapped back from his rambling thoughts as Trent then slowly, and downright deliberately, bent over to pick it up.

"Y-you're right, I w-wouldn't mind t-that at all," he stammered, rubbing lightly on his sore chest. "By the way, that was a great workout last night. I'm feeling it for sure."

"Already? Mission accomplished then," Trent said proudly. "I suspect you're going to be feeling a lot of things this week, J,"

Jonny sighed, and it came out much louder than expected. Becoming flushed across his clean-shaven face, he wished that there was something he could do to show Trent his appreciation or at least save himself from the embarrassing moment.

Trent chuckled, white smile beaming as he made his way into the kitchen. Tossing the bag onto the tiles adjacent to the dishwasher, he leaned up against the same counter where the two had prepared their pre-workout shakes earlier. Spotting a stray sprinkling of powder, Trent passed a single finger through it, using his broad tongue to lick it off.

Jonny nearly fainted at the sight and memory of their close encounter.

"Damn me and my rules, eh?" Trent said achingly as he finished, the bulges in both their shorts protesting as well.

Jonny could only manage a curt nod, his eyes following Trent as he squatted to remove their dirty shaker cups from the bag. His ass was so perfect, each sweeping cheek threatening to burst out of his shorts as he loaded the dishwasher.

Damn, Jonny thought, admiring pure masculinity in motion.

Trent knew that he was being watched. After all, this wasn't his first rodeo toying with tricks. However, the chemistry he could feel percolating for Jonny certainly muddied the water (although it was safe to assume Trent would *never* use that word to describe what was going on between them).

"So," Jonny began, having regained some measure of composure, "are we doing the same thing again tonight? At Swole? We did chest, so what are we going to be working out?"

"Whoa there, eager beaver," Trent replied as he stood all the way back up. "You're so full of questions for a fuck buddy!"

Jonny slid back into his apologetic self, eyes falling to the floor even as they passed Trent's tented shorts. As Trent's hands planted themselves firmly on his own hips with his head shaking, Jonny's shoulders slumped, causing his oversized tank top to droop even more.

"Jesus, you need to work on knowing when I. Am. Joking," Trent said.

"That would be a lot easier if your face matched your mood," Jonny replied.

Trent made a sound halfway between a laugh and a scoff.

"Can't be predictable now, can I? That would mean ol' Trent Cassidy would develop a rep for being rusty."

With Jonny still hunched, Trent slipped over to him. The twenty-one-year old's head floated just above Trent's furry chest, and he stood so close that his breath billowed through Jonny's hair. Dropping his head, Trent inhaled deeply, then let out a sputtering exhale.

"Look, about… us. I have no idea what's going on. Like I told you on the way back here, most other dudes would have been gone long before ever setting foot in my house – the rules you know so well now. Each time it's quite literally get a pump, do some ruthless grinding, then adios amigo until next time. But… Hell… I don't know if it's because you're here visiting and have a way into my haven but," Trent sighed one more time, "you've gotten into my head Jonny-boy and I'm not a hundred percent sure I like it."

Jonny was a mixed bag of assorted emotions.

"Good Lord man, you look like you're about to puke. It doesn't mean I don't like you," Trent clarified, grabbing each of Jonny's shoulders. He could feel the little guy trembling like a leaf in a stiff breeze. "If that were the case, I would have beaten the shit out of you earlier when I thought you were trespassing, instead of taking you to Swole to train."

Jonny didn't laugh at the joke.

Trent grumbled.

"I'm still planning to see you the rest of this week for our sessions, that is if you still want them. And I think we've well established that you're *not* one of my regular fuck buddies."

"Well *that's* reassuring," Jonny said unenthusiastically.

Trent scowled.

"Ugh, it's just that I don't want to assume there's anything …"

"More? To us?" Jonny cut in, lifting his head so their gazes met. He could see an internal battle raging within Trent's eyes.

"Honestly, yeah."

"Look, I told you I'm not looking for anything like that either," Jonny said briskly. "Anyway, I've known you for less than a day and when I last checked this story isn't a fairy tale…"

"Far from it," Trent said as he nodded, but the action was clearly hollow. Internally, he just chalked these recent happenings up to lust – the always reliable and easy excuse – and tucked any further notions about Jonny and him having anything more, into the back of his mind.

Still ahold of Jonny, Trent glanced outside the window. It was notably lighter.

"J, what's the time?"

Jonny pulled out his phone and pressed the home button. The screen lit up, indicating that it was nearly six-thirty.

"Damn," Trent said, "time flies. The sun will be coming up soon, and both of us need to get a little rest before tackling our Sundays."

"You're right," Jonny said, still with disappointment. Despite their exchange, he liked his close-up view of Trent's fuzzy face. "Guess that means I should head upstairs. Jared wants to do some surfing today."

Trent leaned forward, hovering beside Jonny's ear.

"Not that he's very good at it," he whispered.

"Neither am I," Jonny replied with a light laugh, pausing as the fine hairs of Trent's beard stroked his cheek.

Trent pulled himself back, the look in his eyes was the same as the feeling in Jonny's chest.

Jonny stood on his tiptoes and lifted his chin, his lips approaching Trent's. But instead of meeting, they pressed against a thick finger that appeared in between.

"Remember J, there are rules here," Trent replied, pushing Jonny away with his finger before moving them to grab Jonny on that smooth chin of his. "Don't mope too much, boyo. We'll have another chance for that and more tonight. Now go on, get a couple hours of sleep before Jared

wakes up and has you both turned into shark bait."

THE NEXT THREE HOURS PASSED far too quickly for

Jonny, who spent most of it tossing and turning on a squeaky, flattened

futon. Sleep was evasive, and the noise didn't help, but his brain was set on

going a thousand miles an hour. It leaped from thoughts about his feelings

for Trent – which were very confusing in their own right – over to the

wildly erotic chest session they'd just had, then finally on how he was

going to handle Jared for the remainder of the week.

This was supposed to be nice and simple; a relaxing getaway, Jonny

thought, though he suspected Jared didn't invite him up just for a week of

guiltless bro-time at bonfires and frat parties.

No, Jared had been hinting quite strongly at his own swelling

feelings, especially in the flood of text messages he'd been sending over the

last two weeks, punctuated with strings of kissing and heart emojis.

After Jonny had broken up with his mentally abusive ex, he didn't

want to leap into another relationship. Who would want to chance that

sort of heavy emotional drain coming back into their life? However, what

Jonny *did* like was the attention, and so for both the right and wrong reasons, he kept the fires of flirting stoked but Jared at arm's length, using the distance between them to his advantage.

Now that he was in Logan, that defense was gone, and before the two of them had really gotten a chance to talk, Trent had swooped in, knocked Jonny off his feet with his muscles, and plowed his great big dick into Jonny's tight ass.

"What an absolute cluster," Jonny moaned, flinging a pillow over his face.

While smothered, he heard some scuffling down the hall, then weighty footsteps as they trundled up to his sparsely furnished guest room. The door was ajar.

"Hey, you up?" said an incredibly deep but groggy voice through the gap.

"Yeah, I'm up," Jonny answered; it was Jared. Throwing the pillow to the side and sitting up slightly, he yawned loudly. "Sorry, I didn't get much sleep."

"I bet," was the short reply.

Jonny could sense something was amiss.

"I'm gonna snag some water," Jared said after a moment of silence, "and head over to Café Lola's. You game? It's bottomless brunch."

"Sure, sure," Jonny replied, tossing away the covers. He clambered to his feet, and as he stretched, it dawned on him that he was still dressed in Trent's borrowed gym clothes.

Oh gosh, did Jared notice? Would he recognize the clothes? The voice in his Jonny's head was timid at first, soon booming. *Of course, you idiot, they're gym clothes for crying out loud! Not to mention you are the farthest thing in existence from a gym rat!*

Swinging his gaze toward the door, Jonny saw Jared start to lumber off; he hadn't said anything more. Jonny relaxed until he heard a very definite 'huh.'

Jonny was single and shouldn't feel like he'd stepped into a large pile of shit, yet there he was, apparently up to his knees in it. Hurriedly switching out the oversized tank top for a more fitting tee, Jonny anxiously followed, making his way for the door, down the steps, and into the kitchen. As he rounded the corner, Jonny saw Jared standing by the fridge, back toward him with a large cup in hand. He took a second to study him; the situation reversed from how he met Trent earlier that morning.

Jared was shorter than Trent (and slightly taller than Jonny was) but much beefier, his back and shoulders resembling a muscle-bound cobra.

"You done gawking?" Jared said without turning.

"Oh! Good morning," Jonny said over the sound of ice cubes falling into the plastic cup.

Jared let out a grunt as he scratched his hair, long enough to be drawn up into a mini man-bun if he wanted, but thankfully those dark brown locks were kept free and untamed.

"Not so much of a good one, then?" Jonny continued, taking a seat on one of the three barstools that lined the backside of the counter.

Drink poured, Jared turned around slowly, his suave face and blue eyes staring right at Jonny. They bore into him. Jonny wanted to look away.

"You tell me," Jared said as he inspected Jonny's clothes, noticing he'd changed. Taking a big gulp, a stream of water flowed down his scruffy neck. It continued between the slabs of his square chest, then down a deep chasm along the center of his abs, until arriving at a pair of snug red sweatpants that clung to every inch of his three powerful legs.

"W-what do you mean?" Jonny replied, wondering if this was the bullshit Trent had mentioned. It didn't take long to confirm that this was exactly the case.

"Nice outfit change," Jared answered, followed by another hydrating gulp.

"Oh," Jonny said as if caught with his hands in places they shouldn't have been (though Jared knew Trent, and it was *his* hands that often found their way inside inappropriate places).

"Yeah... oh."

Jared casually strolled up to the other side of the counter and set his cup down. Drops of condensation splattered across the marble while others trickled down the sides of the black plastic like nervous sweat.

"I just have one question for you."

Jonny felt uncomfortable; it was the cold of Jared's stare.

"Trent?"

Jonny sighed, Jared taking that to mean yes and suddenly he flew off the handle.

"Good fucking GOD, can that asshole ever just leave my shit alone..." Jared snarled. His chest was heaving, one of his hands drawn up into a tense fist.

Jonny watched the reaction unfold, trying to find the right moment so he could say something, wondering the whole time if he should.

"Are you okay?" he asked, plucking up the courage.

"Do I look it?" Jared's words lashed. "I swear that douche is always sticking his dick where it doesn't belong."

Jonny blushed guiltily.

"W-what's wrong with a little workout?" he threw out, hoping the innocence of his tone would stick.

"Really?" Jared replied skeptically. "*Really*? You're going to stand there telling me that Mr. Casanova Cassidy himself just worked out with you, after hours in that gym of his no less, with absolutely none of the fringe benefits he's got a reputation for?"

"Well, no, but…"

"Exactly!" Jared snapped again, counting along his fingers as he said, "Butts. Asses. Big dicks. Fists. Hell, even pussy. You name it, and the fucker's probably done it."

Jonny could not only sense the longstanding angst between them both, but he could see it also, straining in every tense fiber of Jared's body.

"You know brother, maybe it wasn't such a good idea for me to come up this week," Jonny murmured, rising from the stool. "I'm going to go pack and hop on one of the buses tomorrow morning and..."

"What? No!" Jared exclaimed; it was as if a calming switch flipped.

"Well, there's obviously some issues between you and Trent that I've landed right smack in the middle of and..."

Jared wet his lips and exhaled, reaching for his water.

"Yeah, there are. Look, I'm sorry man. What... and who you do on your own time is none of my business. I couldn't care less." Jared said casually.

Jonny suspected he *did* care, otherwise he wouldn't have sent the text he did just yesterday, which said: *I'm so glad it's finally time and can't wait to see you! Have a safe trip.*

Jonny recalled all the damn hearts that seemed to replace the punctuation. A part of him felt guilty that he'd jumped at the chance to spend time with Trent before Jared. Another part of him wadded the guilt up and chucked it in the trash, thinking that it was a great time.

Jared saw the thoughtful look in Jonny's eyes.

"I just wanted to spend some time getting to know you more, preferably without interference."

"Well we have today, man," Jonny said reassuringly.

"I know we do; you're not getting out of surfing that easily. It'll be a very good time, but admittedly I'm concerned about tonight."

"Why's that?"

Jared pointed toward the hall leading to the master bedroom.

"Ah, that," Jonny replied.

"Yeah. Are you planning to workout with him again?"

Jonny felt embarrassed talking so casually about sex with Jared, but answered, "Yes. We're supposed to be training again tonight."

Jared let out a slight chuckle as he downed the rest of his water. Placing the cup in the sink, he propped himself up against the counter and folded his arms.

"That almost makes it sound innocent," he said, "but, most ordinary people work out during regular hours. He's just going to fuck you again."

Wow, blunt much? Maybe I want him to, Jonny thought, knowing better than to say it.

"I just don't want to see you hurt," Jared added with genuine care. "Just be cautious with who you're dealing with, *especially* when it comes to your feelings. Trent has a knack for playing with them, especially if it gets

him what he wants."

Jonny took those words to heart, even though Trent's rang out as

he did.

You've gotten into my head Jonny-boy...

Surely, he wouldn't be feeding him a line just for a hole to stick his

cock in? It felt more real than that.

"Besides," Jared continued, "you're a good guy, and I'm not going

to let Trent stop me from having a great time this week with a great

friend."

"Me either," Jonny replied, smiling.

"Well, enough depressing talk! Let's get on with the day.

Bottomless brunch awaits!"

"What exactly is that?" Jonny asked as Jared worked his way

around the counter toward the stairs. His eyes dawdled on Jared's ass, the

red sweats like a second skin.

"It means for twenty-five bucks you can eat anything off the menu,

in any order, in any amount. Why do you think I'm this big?" he replied,

flexing a bicep.

"Sounds amazing."

"Trust me, it is! Okay, I'll go ahead and shower, unless you want to conserve some water now?"

"Maybe later this week?" Jonny laughed.

Jared smirked, and with a wink, he was up the stairs with more speed than a man his size should be able to muster.

As the thundering footsteps subsided, Jonny looked one last time down the hall toward Trent's room. This whole situation was so strange, and he didn't like playing both sides of the fence, but having never faced this sort of thing before – two outrageously gorgeous guys primping and preening over him like a prize – he was just cruising along to see what happened.

Then his mind started to throw curve balls…

Should I just go ahead and march down that hall to end it with Trent?

You've seen that guy, right? You want him mad or sending a fist your way?

Should I tell Jared to take a hike at brunch?

And ruin such a great friendship? Hell no.

Fine! Should I just be a man-whore for the week, get fucked by both, and see who does the better job?

Bingo! I see nothing wrong with that.

"I see everything wrong with it," Jonny muttered, running his hands through his hair as he stood there alone in his woes. "Talk about first world problems!"

Jonny knew that he wasn't that great of a catch, looking in the mirror daily reminded him of that sobering fact; the guys those two could land with a snap of their muscled fingers made up twenty of him.

So, it was then that he reluctantly (and totally against his better judgment) decided on the latter. It was the easiest route to take, all things considered. However, that assumed Jared and Trent wouldn't kill each other in the process, and something told Jonny as he looked at himself in a hall mirror that it was a very good possibility.

CHAPTER 2

BOTTOMLESS BRUNCH

THE SUN GLINTED OFF A PASSING car, causing Jared to shield his eyes.

"Hey, Tiffany?" he said to the blonde waitress, whose perkiness would be enough to make the grumpiest customer cheery, if her matching breasts failed to do the job. "Could you be a doll and close those blinds for me?"

"Sure thing," she replied in an effervescent tone, fluttering over to the windows. After a quick turn of the wand, the sun disappeared and the vibrant interior of Café Lola came back into view.

Spring break might have had the place crammed full of youngsters, Jared sitting at a small two-person table, but it was a charming place nonetheless. Bright colors and paintings adorned the walls while the scents of exotic ingredients mixed pleasantly with similar music in the air.

"Ah, that's much better," Jared said, taking a sip of pulpy orange juice as she returned. "Jonny, you decide what you're getting first?"

"There's so much on here," Jonny replied, his overloaded eyes scanning four columns of offerings. "These are small plates, right?"

Tiffany bobbed her head, and her entire body followed.

"Yep! Appetizer sized. Once you're finished, you can order more, and we'll keep bringing them out until you burst!"

"I hope it doesn't come to that," he replied, stopping at the fish tacos. "I think I'll try these, along with the... hmmm... how is the French toast?"

"It's excellent," Tiffany replied, "one of my favorite things on the menu."

"I'll take one of those then," Jonny said.

"I'll take one also," Jared added, "and a double order of sesame steak skewers."

"You got it, boys," she said, bouncing away. She glanced over her shoulder while twizzling her pen's cap playfully between her teeth.

"Well, well, someone likes us," Jared whispered, involuntarily flexing his back. "But she would say the French toast was her favorite thing, wouldn't she? I bet they have to say that regardless of what's asked about."

"You mean she likes *you*," Jonny replied sensitively. "Who wouldn't though, that v-neck is so small you've not only got people covered who like to ogle studs, but who like to admire toddlers as well."

Jared looked at Jonny, directly across from him, and observed his nerdy outfit: an off-white *Pokémon* tee and skinny jeans. He thought it suited Jonny much better than a jumbo tank top and musty gym shorts. Since it was truly 'him' and that's what made it great.

"It doesn't matter too much does it, considering she's not our type?" Jared answered grumpily. "Besides, I happen to find shirts this size *very* comfortable."

"You would. So, does …"

Jonny suddenly stopped; he was about to mention Trent.

Jared wasn't stupid, though in the interest of keeping things cool he tried to hide his annoyance. That was difficult at best.

"Speaking of *jerks*," he said, squashing an obstinate silence that started to form while threatening to launch an argument, "is the ex-boyfriend totally out of the picture now?"

"Fred?" Jonny answered, relieved Jared wasn't pressing him on Trent, but his face cringed, and lips curled anyway from the mere mention of his ex's name. "Yeah, that bastard's history as of the middle of last week."

Jared looked relieved, though it could be read as pleased.

"Good, you deserve much better than that loser."

"Do I?"

"What?" Jared asked. He was expecting agreement and didn't know quite what to say.

"Sometimes I wonder if I do deserve better…" Jonny continued, melancholy. "It feels like my lot in life. As I work my butt off in all sorts of this things – trying to be successful at them – love, classes, you name it, the only success I seem to be reaping is getting shafted in the end. Not the good kind either. Geez, I swear it feels like I have 'fuck me over' tattooed on my forehead. The very least these people could do is have the courtesy to lube up beforehand."

Jared pretended to inspect the area in detail, complete with an invisible magnifying glass.

"Nope, no letters as far as I can see," he replied, and Jonny smiled. "Look, all this hard work will all pay off in the end. Life has hurdles, and everyone is different. You're just facing more now rather than later, I'm sure of it."

A supportive hand made its way from Jared's side of the table, navigating napkins, flatware, and condiments before settling on top of Jonny's.

Jonny's eyes flicked downward.

"Jared, I…"

"You don't think I know that you've been keeping me at bay?"

"It's all the hearts," Jonny said half-laughing.

"Yeah, I love those, probably too much eh?" Jared smirked. "But seriously, I can't blame you for needing your space. I told you back at the house that you're a good guy, one of the best I know, and Fred definitely did a number on you up here."

Jared tapped his temple with his free hand, and Jonny looked off to a distant part of the café.

"You're hurt from those experiences," Jared continued. "Anybody would be, but I'm not going to lie: I like you, a lot. I just want you to know from the bottom of my heart to the top of your aching one: I'm here for you, should you need me."

Jonny pulled his hand away, complicated feelings and thoughts raging once more.

Why is this shit never easy?

Instead of withdrawing further, Jonny placed his hand back on top of Jared's and rubbed it with his thumb.

"Thank you," he replied, "it's great knowing that I have you as a friend."

"I could be more than a friend if you wanted…" he hinted, smiling.

"I… I will think about it," Jonny answered, his mind already contemplating how much harder the week was going to be on him than he thought.

"That's all I ask," Jared replied as Tiffany returned with their first round of food.

CHAPTER 3

THE CARB UP

"I FEEL LIKE A PIECE of meat," Jonny said as he bobbed around in his seat, unrelenting potholes seeming to have multiplied during the day.

He'd been talking with Trent about his day, which had been going great with Jared until half an hour ago.

Expecting a snarky reply from Trent, Jonny was surprised when he didn't get one.

"You pretty much are," Trent replied bluntly.

"Thanks," Jonny said disapprovingly.

"You're welcome. I wouldn't dwell on it or worry too much, though; Jared will get over it. He always does."

Jonny slowly turned his head toward Trent, placing a hand on his jeans-covered thigh and giving it a light squeeze.

Earlier, Jared had a confrontation with Trent and suffice to say: it wasn't pretty. He was trying to get Jonny to go with him to a party over at a local frat house, but Jonny had already committed to another workout session with Trent (for the entire week, in fact). So, instead of things going smoothly, that's when the posturing between the two muscle-heads escalated.

Trent insisted Jonny wasn't missing out and Jared was using the day's fun in an attempt to guilt Jonny into going to the party while telling Trent to keep his dick zipped up in his pants.

To Jonny, the arguing made him feel like he was smack in the middle of his old relationship again and he just wanted to tell them both to fuck off, pack his bags, and call a cab to the bus station.

But, he didn't, Trent's fucking lustful stare anchoring his feet to the floor of the house while Jared's friendly face did the same.

Jonny was torn (and shouldn't have been), ultimately deciding on his original commitment to Trent. Jared wasn't happy about it at all, storming off to the party by himself without another word. The look of disappointment on his face, along with the echoing sting of the slamming door managed to stick with Jonny.

"I'm sorry about all that back at the house," Trent continued, drawing Jonny's attention back to the present. "What you've been seeing between us is nothing new. It fucking sucks balls, and I guess the fact you're a mutual buddy is amplifying his tirades."

Jonny could only focus on one word in that entire sentence.

"Buddy?" he spat.

"Dude, I wasn't talking about *that* kind of buddy," Trent was quick to say defensively. "On second thought, aren't you both kinds now? Making you a bi-buddy, or bi-bud? Which do you prefer Jonny-boy?"

"Ugh! There's the real Trent; knew he wouldn't be gone for long. Away with your truths," Jonny barked, yanking his hand away from Trent's leg only to have it snatched back into position. He turned his head and looked out of the window with a small smile.

A few blissful minutes went by.

"Hey, Trent…"

"Yeah, *buddy?*"

"You're hilarious… not. I was just wondering if we were still heading over to Swole now; I don't remember seeing any of this stuff we're passing, but I guess you might have had me a little distracted the first time."

"Seems like I'm doing that now," Trent observed, spotting a tent in Jonny's shorts. "Tell little John it'll be playtime soon enough, but damn you're observant. The Summerset Center is still a bit further north; I'm taking you west for something big to eat."

"Eat?" Jonny asked with surprise, his head spinning back around while flashes of steak skewers came back to haunt him. "So, we aren't working out then?"

"Oh, you bet that beautiful ass of yours we are," Trent replied. "I'm not letting you off that easily. In fact, I think I was far too gentle with you for chest, so we're hitting the other end of the spectrum: body part most hate so much they skip working out entirely."

"I'm almost afraid to ask what that is," Jonny said, still sore across both his chest and lower body.

"Legs," Trent replied with an evil smile.

Jonny looked down to his hand which was still caressing that massive hunk of meat Trent had as a limb.

"Oh shit," he mumbled, Trent chuckling.

"Gosh, you're so worrisome. I'm not going to force you to move the same amount of weight I do, but it's still not going to be easy."

"Not sure I want to do it now."

"You want the rewards, don't you?"

Jonny nodded eagerly, followed by a hard swallow.

"Well then, in order to do it right, we have to get fueled up properly," Trent said. "Which is why I'm taking you for something to eat."

Jonny still thought the whole idea was odd.

"Not every meathead thinks the same way," Trent continued, donning his personal trainer's hat. "Some nut jobs train fasted, but I'm a big believer in carbing up before leg and back days since they're heavier lifts." He smirked. "The kind you should like: *brutal*."

Parts of Jonny tensed up, while others quivered with the thought.

"Here I thought I did well enough to get through that chest workout, and you're telling me that it's going to get worse."

"Haha, you did do well," Trent replied. "Don't go doubting that one bit, but yeah, it's going to be worse for you tonight and in a way, much better."

"If you say so. It sounds horrifying."

Jonny didn't know if it was butterflies in his stomach or just the thought of eating something substantial that late (spurred by his gluttonous session with Jared) but he was put off by the idea.

"Sounds to me like you're just asking to be sick," Jonny said, hoping the thought of vomit would steer Trent toward Swole. But this was Trent Cassidy he was talking to, and Jonny should have known better by now.

"Puking on leg day?" Trent replied. "That's the ultimate badge of honor."

"Of course it is," Jonny said, thinking that gym rats were some of the hottest, yet strangest people around.

Trent flicked the turn signal and spun the wheel, his '69 Charger gliding across the lanes into a parking lot, which was surprisingly busy for ten o'clock.

Jonny leaned forward as the car came to a stop between two pickup trucks, looking at the packed building ahead, the lights of a garish sign dancing across the glass.

"The Lard Have Mercy?" he said sardonically. "I swear Trent, folks in this town have the weirdest names for places."

"There's nothing weird about LHM," Trent retorted, serious as if his mother was slandered. "Besides, it's a well-known chain that started in Houston, so don't go blaming Logan for that."

"*I've* never heard of it."

"That's because you've been sheltered in that tiny town you live in, but you're about to get acquainted with some of the best burgers around."

"We could have just gone to Mc –"

Trent's hand shot up, a single finger raised.

"No. Fucking. Way. That place isn't in the same category; you'll see." Trent's voice shifted from admonishment to admiration. "This place has the best food and some of the largest burgers in the country. Heard stories of some guy named Gage in Texas, ate the Colossal King in less than ten minutes. That's like nearly two pounds of beef. Shit, I've never made it past the Royal Triple Decker. Bet his pump was immense."

"And I bet the toilet screamed immensely too," Jonny chuckled. He liked seeing Trent's enthusiasm; it suited him. Hopefully, it was something he would see more. "Okay, you've convinced me. Just be sure you wait until later before you go and have an orgasm unless this Gage does it for you."

Trent grabbed the door handle and popped it open, letting some of the warm night air slip into the cab.

"Please. I thought you knew me by now. Just for that, you're going to make sure I cum twice tonight."

Jonny liked the sound of that threat, opening his door and easing his way outside. Trent wasn't far behind and together, they both made their way to the entrance.

JONNY SAT WITH HIS EYES wide open, the collection of plates laid out in front of them glistening with grease and smelling divine. It was, in a word: heaven.

The joint was extremely busy and full of cheers and good times, spring break contributing a lot to that, plus the extended hours for the week.

Trent was a beast, shoveling fries and bites of eggy patties into his mouth like a front loader while managing to keep his beard pristine. Jonny, on the other hand, pecked at his quarter-pounder like a pigeon.

"We aren't leaving until you finish that," Trent said with his mouth stuffed, swallowing a straw full of water to wash it down. "You are gonna need the energy."

Jonny took a big bite, grease dribbling down his chin into the napkin unfolded across his lap. Trent's eyes followed it, and Jonny smirked, taking another mouthful. More grease stained the napkin below the table.

"Liking what you see?" Jonny asked.

"More like what I can't see right now," Trent replied, his mischievous eyes darting over to a lone saucer on his right. On it was a single, unadorned hotdog bun.

Jonny eyed it, too.

"That was a strange thing to order," he said, considering the rest of the plates were loaded down. "I thought you'd have gotten a hot dog with it."

Trent smiled as if waiting for that as a signal. He looked around and took his hands off the burger, lowering them both beneath the table.

Watching him fidget as if handling a whopper, Jonny rose in his seat to get a better view.

Trent's look was pure sin, his hands full of hard cock, the tip glistening.

Jonny fell back onto his side of the stiff booth.

"Are you serious right now?" Jonny whispered harshly. "Have you seen how many people are in here? Someone is going to see you!"

Trent shrugged, moving one of his hands down the thick shaft and back up again. Using his thumb, he rubbed the slick precum over his head and let out a little moan, generating more. Reaching for the hot dog bun, a long gossamer strand stretched in between.

Holy shit, Jonny thought. *This is so wrong!*

And he liked every fucking second of it.

Grabbing the bun, Trent brought it down to his lap where he unfolded it, wrapping his stiff dick with the soft bread.

"I'm ready," he said to Jonny.

"W-what? Ready for what?"

"I told you, *you're* getting me off twice tonight."

Jonny's heart began beating faster, his eyes scanning the room. He was sure the couple across from them knew what was going on. Maybe the woman over at the counter. Or the man just off and behind him to the left.

He couldn't breathe, especially when his gaze returned to Trent.

"Now," Trent said. "Take off your shoes."

Jonny hesitated, but as Trent leaned forward, growling, he

complied. Slipping out of his sneakers, Jonny wiggled his sock-clad toes.

"Now, bring them up here," Trent ordered.

Jonny eased himself down in the booth, lifting his legs into Trent's

lap. He felt his rough hands grab hold of his ankles, pushing his feet closer

together until they met the bun. Trent then started to move them up and

down, the bun sliding along his unyielding shaft.

"That's it, Jonny-boy," Trent said with a slight rasp. "Work it."

Jonny was sure someone was watching, he could feel eyes on him.

There was no tablecloth, their wicked activity exposed for anyone who

happened to look in their direction.

"Fuck whoever sees," Trent said, noting Jonny's distractions.

"You're attention. On me. Now."

Jonny gulped, focusing on his movement along Trent's dick. It felt

incredibly awkward yet hot as fuck. He added a slight twist to each up and

down stroke, Trent obviously satisfied.

The precum started to gush, flowing down into the now soggy bun. Jonny didn't care, he kept churning, cranking moan after pleasurable moan from his trainer. Then it dawned on him: he was in control at that moment.

Hearing distant murmurs, Jonny closed his eyes and carried on, forgetting that he was in a crowded restaurant while changing rhythm unpredictably, ecstasy surging into Trent's aching loins.

"Oh fuck," Trent uttered, long and agonizingly slow. "You're fucking good at... oh, fuck!"

Jonny could tell Trent was close, his feet now up against raw cock as he continued to stroke Trent off.

"Yeah, you like that big guy?" Jonny muttered.

"Fuck yeah I do. Oh God, I'm about to... oh yeah, you've done it. I'm about to cum."

Jonny opened his eyes, the feeling of Trent's dick causing his own cock to drool the entire time, the scene in his shorts a slick mess. He could feel Trent stiffening, throbbing, convulsing as ropes of streaming white splattered against his dark tank top.

Trent was panting heavily, sweat beaded on his brow.

Glancing at the couple across from them, Jonny spotted the man looking in their direction. He made a subtle thumbs-up gesture before returning his attention to his girlfriend who, surprisingly, hadn't noticed a thing. Amused and somewhat in disbelief, Jonny looked back at Trent; his shirt was disastrous like a large napkin smothered in greasy stains.

"Good job, Jonny-boy," Trent said, his beard finally dirty. "Number one down; one more to go."

Sitting upright, Jonny was rather proud of himself, but he didn't get much of a chance to think about it before their waiter returned. His heart fluttered as the waiter glanced disapprovingly at Trent's shirt, and he prepared himself to be thrown out of the place.

"My goodness you must have hated the food; you're quite the messy eater, aren't you?" the waiter said with a titter. "Sauce and grease are everywhere."

Jonny laughed along with him while Trent cleared away the stray sauce from his beard.

"I'm the messiest of them all," he said smugly, looking devilishly at Jonny. "I think we are ready for the check please."

CHAPTER 4

ASS TO GRASS

"I STILL CANNOT BELIEVE YOU," Jonny said, head shaking as the two pulled into the Summerset Center.

"Just being me," Trent said assertively. "What I can't believe is you didn't even finish that little bitty burger. The thing should be on the kid's menu."

"And you're just going to work out as if you didn't just eat the entire adult menu?"

Trent switched off the engine and looked right at Jonny.

"You bet," he said, lifting a new tank top he had changed into. His abs, on the other hand, looked unchanged.

"Jesus, you don't even have a food baby," Jonny said, reaching out to feel Trent's stomach; it was as hard as ever, each ridge demanding to be touched at least once. Maybe twice (especially the lower ones). "Dammit, I really hate your genetics."

"My other tank top does too," he smirked. "Come on, squats are calling."

Squats, Jonny thought. The name itself was dirty, but he was excited to find out what Trent's spin on the night would be. If it was anything like last time, traditional was not the word to apply to any of this.

The two got out of the car, Trent working his way in ahead of Jonny. He didn't mind being left to follow again, appreciating the persistent view of Trent's ass as it swished hypnotically in those shorts.

"You know, I just realized the highly appropriate color of your sign," Jonny observed, the red lights of the gym's thick lettering calling out like a beacon of sin in the night.

"Mhmm," Trent answered as he opened the door and switched off the alarm. "Care to get the lights again?"

"Sure," Jonny said, heading over to the right to flip the switch.

Once again, the lights flickered to life, and Trent's private playground appeared out of the darkness.

"Remember him?" Trent asked as they walked through toward the locker rooms, pointing in the direction of the leg area on the left. A squat rack sat in the center. "We're gonna get some work done on that later."

Jonny eyed the machine, recalling it from last time. Tonight, its black metal frame looked far more intimidating.

"Yup, remember *brutal* is the word. Nothing like the tanning booth…"

Jonny trembled with good memories, looking over at the booth's locked door.

"And no worries for you this time on us being interrupted by Lisa." Trent stopped just ahead of the locker room door, putting a hand on Jonny's shoulder before sliding it down the length of his upper arm. "You're *all mine.*"

With that, he grabbed hold and guided Jonny into the room, its gray walls and blue lockers welcoming them back. Tossing his bag on one of the wooden benches in the middle he turned, pushing Jonny up against a bank of cold metal with one hand, slamming the other next to his head. Before Jonny could even say a word, Trent had moved in to kiss him, the two locking lips for a couple of minutes.

"You should change your shorts; still messy from the restaurant," Trent said, pulling away just as quickly as he'd rushed in, leaving Jonny wobbly against the locker. He rifled through his gym bag, tossing over a clean pair.

"Do you always keep spare clothes in your gym bag?"

Trent looked at Jonny saying, "I swear, once I think that you've finally worked out the kind of guy I am, you prove me wrong. What I don't have in here, I have in some of those locker's you're trembling against."

"Sorry, it's just cold."

"Yeah, sure it is," Trent said as he watched Jonny change, his dick flopping around as he pulled the new pair up. "Didn't look all that cold to me."

"Whatever. So, are you going to change?"

Without another word, Trent lowered his onion skin shorts, his massive meat dangling heavily. Walking over to the locker next to Jonny, he reached in and pulled out a pair of sweat shorts that looked amazing on him.

"You really do have all this down to a science, don't you?"

"Fuck yes I do," Trent replied and with a wink added, "I even pay Lisa extra to do my gym laundry."

Jonny couldn't manage anything but a light smile, shaking his head in disbelief.

"I told you she knows me well," Trent said. "Now, help me get these on."

Jonny blinked, half expecting to get another show from behind, full of tight hamstrings and sculpted ass.

"Wait, what?"

"You heard me," he answered, dropping the shorts to the floor and placing one foot in them. "I need some help getting them on."

Jonny sunk to his knees, the tile floor uncomfortable. Nonetheless, he guided Trent's foot into one of the leg holes, followed by the other. As he lifted them up and over his calves, he could feel something tapping against the top of his head. Raising his gaze, he saw that it was Trent, slapping his semi-hard cock against him.

Continuing, Jonny stretched the shorts over Trent's mammoth thighs, and once the elastic was just beneath his crotch, Jonny stopped. Leaning forward, he buried his nose in Trent's bull-sized balls, spreading those two generous orbs to each side as he inhaled, bathing them with his tongue at the same time. The powerful, masculine scent spurred him on, and he lifted the shorts some more. They soon covered his balls, riding higher up the shaft. Jonny used his tongue to pave a smooth path all the way up those nine inches to tip, where a shiny reward waited. Jonny lapped it up amidst several moans, sucking on the head to draw out every remaining drop before sealing the package away.

"That's a good boy," Trent said boldly, pushing Jonny's face into his shorts. "Now it's time to get started."

JONNY WAS ALREADY ABOUT TO lose it by the time they'd even made it to the gym floor, Trent heading down a little way before turning right into the leg room.

Shit, I hope I make it through tonight, he said to himself as he stepped onto the spongy mats, worried that if Trent so much as looked at him the wrong way he would cum instantly.

That feeling went away as Jonny surveyed the room. There were metal dumbbells along the wall to the right, but what drew his eyes was all the daunting equipment. Plate-loaded machines (the squat rack, a Smith machine, and a leg press to name a few) stood front and center while other machines (for leg extension, curls, and the like) were to his left. Between the metal jungle was a series of weight trees, each ladened with iron plates ranging from five up to forty-five pounds.

"Well, it's official," Jonny said. "I've already shit myself."

Trent laughed as he made way over to the leg extensions.

"We'll start here," he said, repositioning the backrest and taking a seat. The taunt vinyl squeaked as Trent adjusted himself and grabbing the pin, he placed it all the way down the stack. Positioning the padded lower bar just above his ankles, he said, "I normally do sets of single then double-legged extensions, but tonight we'll only go through four sets of doubles, okay?"

"Don't tell me you're already going easy?"

"No, but you should consider it a thank you for helping me so well with my shorts."

Trent then set about cranking out his set, scowling by the time he was on the last few reps. With a pained groan and a loud *clang*, he finished, legs throbbing as he struggled to stand.

"Your turn," he said, pointing at the seat.

Jonny took his time, feeling like he was climbing into an electric chair. The feeling didn't subside as he raised the pin to about eighty pounds (Trent was doing two-hundred-fifty).

The first few raises weren't all that bad until Trent instructed him to, "Squeeze those quads at the top."

That's when the searing burn started, increasing with each repetition. It was painful, but also somewhat pleasing, particularly when Trent placed a hand on one of Jonny's thighs to make sure he was doing as he was told.

Jonny floundered.

"I didn't say stop," Trent snarled. "Give me two more... that's it... one... and... good."

When the weights came crashing down, releasing Jonny from their grasp, his legs were tingling, and he had great difficulty standing.

"What were you saying about me going easy, bro? That was just set number one," Trent said as he watched Jonny woozily brace himself on a nearby piece of equipment. "We still have three more to go."

With rugged grunts, some yells, and a few cuss words, the two of them made their way through the rest of the leg extensions. By the end, Trent's legs had lost some of their definition but were unbelievably swollen and veiny as a result. Jonny tried his best to trace all the crossing lines with his eyes, but there were so many of them that he lost track.

Fuck my life, he thought. *That's hot!*

"You like my personal road maps?" Trent joked as he made his way over to a mat that was typically used for deadlifts. "Use 'em to find your way over here."

"Yeah, they're great," Jonny replied as he wet his lips, watching Trent grab one of the pre-weighted barbells off a pyramidal rack. Even though they weren't working out arms, his seem to be engorged. "I don't know how you don't spend all day looking at yourself in the mirror."

"You flatter me, boyo," Trent said, throwing the bar across his upper back. "Lunges next. Four sets, ten to fifteen reps."

He stepped forward with one leg and plunged, lowering himself until the opposing knee touched the mat. Then, after a brief pause, he pushed himself back up.

Jonny watched, trying to focus on form, but all he could see was Trent's ass popping out like some ripe peach at the bottom and clenching tightly at the top of the movement. Trent repeated the process with the other leg and got into a smooth back and forth rhythm until all fifteen reps per leg were done.

"You made that look really easy," Jonny said, snatching a lighter bar off the same rack to use. Trying to duplicate what he saw Trent doing, Jonny struggled at times to get back off the floor.

"That was a good job for your first try. Just make sure you keep your core tight, and you should be set," Trent noted. "It'll help your form and the ability to get your ass back up."

Jonny breathed heavily while nodding, noticing Trent's shorts were soaked up front.

"Sweating so much already?" he asked playfully.

"It's not sweat," Trent said, dipping into his next set.

Jonny rubbed the back of his neck bashfully until it was his turn again.

Once those draining sets of lunges were out of the way, Trent took Jonny through a round on both the abductor and adductor machines. Typically machines that discouraged eye contact with those using them, Trent and Jonny gave each other sideways glances as their legs spread open in compromising positions.

"Those machines are far more fun with women," Trent said casually, wagging his tongue as he arrived at the lying leg curl machine.

Jonny didn't say anything, putting a thumb in his mouth as he watched Trent getting into position on his stomach. The man set the weight and immediately curled his legs upward.

"Watch my form carefully," he said between grunts and timed breaths. "You're going to have to duplicate it perfectly before we move onto the final routine."

"Seems easy enough," Jonny replied. "I'm am glad we're lying down for these."

Trent answered with a wry smirk, surveying every inch of Jonny as he got into position.

After a few reps with surprisingly good form, Jonny could feel Trent's gaze boring into him again. Out of the corner of an eye, he could see Trent working the front of his shorts, and soon, he had positioned himself mere inches in front of Jonny. That massive cock was struggling to get out of those shorts.

"Don't stop," Trent scolded. "That could be a dangerous thing."

Jonny bowed his head obediently and continued with his sets. That's when he felt Trent's massive weight settle on top of him, that hard dick resting against the back of his head while Trent's hands and face made way for Jonny's ass.

"Keep going," Trent directed, his hands caressing then kneading Jonny's cheeks as they moved his shorts down, exposing his silky, smooth skin.

Trent groaned as he spread those cheeks apart, getting a glimpse of that treasured hole he'd been craving. He brushed his beard along the dividing line, causing Jonny to falter.

"Tsk, tsk. There's that bad form creeping in," Trent grumbled, continuing his bearded assault.

"It's y-your f-fault," Jonny stammered, eyes rolling back into his head. He could barely breathe from the strain of the curls plus Trent's body on top of his.

"Don't blame my facial hair for your hiccups."

Jonny would have retorted, but he could only manage a long moan, the soft bristles surrounding Trent's mouth hovering precariously over his tender breach. He could feel his breath; he was so close.

"Oh... that feels good..." Jonny groaned, feeling a spit-lubed finger circling, then plunging into his depths. It rifled around, seeking his prostrate like a guided missile and once it made contact, Jonny exploded with shuddering grace.

His legs fell, and the weights crashed, Trent adding a second, then a third finger to explore.

"Fuck!" Jonny roared, his dick salivating while trapped between him and the machine's padding. "I'm getting close..."

Trent ignored him, his fingers doing all the answering on his behalf.

"T-Trent, s-stop." Jonny writhed. "I'm... I'm going to..."

The wild scream that followed shook the building, all four of Trent's fingers diving in just as Jonny's dick pumped out hot and sticky pools that drenched his shorts.

Jonny collapsed, the full weight of Trent's sweaty body crushing him.

"Congrats," Trent whispered. "You've earned squat time."

IT TOOK JONNY NEARLY TEN minutes to recuperate now that Trent was off him. The vinyl was almost refreshing against his body, like the cold side of a pillow that had just been flipped over. He could have stayed there for another ten minutes, but something told him that Trent wouldn't be too pleased with that amount of laziness in his gym.

Looking around while still on his belly, Jonny didn't immediately see Trent, but could hear him loading the squat rack. Grudgingly standing, Jonny looked toward the center of the room and saw the big guy putting three forty-five pound plates on one side of the bar, moving on to the other. The weight was impressive, but Trent doing it all stark naked was even more.

"Hey sleepy head," Trent called as the first plate slammed into position. His body didn't even look worn or tired. "All rested up?"

"Yeah," Jonny replied blearily, trying his best to stop himself from yawning, the second plate banging into place helping on that front. "I hope you're not expecting me to lift all that?"

"What, three-forty-five too much for you?" Trent prodded as he shifted the last plate into position, placing a padded cylinder around the middle of the bar afterward. "I figured we could knock my sets out as usual then I could focus on you."

Jonny liked Trent's idea of focusing, moving closer to the squat rack. Looking closer at the setup up, it looked downright scary, like some medieval torture device.

"I don't think I need a spot," Trent said as he positioned himself with the pad across the upper part of his back and his arms out to the sides, grasping the bar. "But be on standby just in case."

"What's that mean?" Jonny asked, completely drawing a blank.

"It means I might need you to help guide me, but I normally do this weight fairly easily for sets of ten."

To his surprise, Jonny started to stir below his shorts again, dick growing at the thought that Trent was about to move weight that was essentially equivalent to more than two of him, across his back.

"You know what would help to motivate me?" Trent asked.

Jonny shook his head rapidly.

"You taking off those clothes."

"Me?" Jonny hesitated.

"Yes you," Trent said. "I swear these sessions are making you deaf. Take them off then step a little over to my right. I want to see you in the mirror as I do these."

Slowly, Jonny took off the tank top, revealing his lean body and when he slid off those tainted shorts, Trent made a distinct grunt as Jonny's growing chub came into view.

Fucking hell, Trent thought as he wiped his lips with a couple of those thick fingers, drooling at the size difference of Jonny's David to his Goliath.

"Much better," Trent said, lifting the weight then stepping back a couple of paces.

Jonny stared in amazement as Trent dropped toward the floor, his ass nearly touching the mat before he strained and shouted back up to the top. Every fiber in his legs jittered with stress as it underwent rep after rep, the fibers being worn and torn to come back bigger and even stronger than before. As Trent pounded through his routine, Jonny's hand gripped the base of his dick and started stroking, getting to full length by the time Trent had finished his third and final set.

"I appreciate that," he said, striding up to Jonny. "A lot."

Taking him into his massive arms, he brought him close and gave him a kiss on the neck, working his way up to his lips. As their chests touched, each could feel the heartbeat of the other, racing in sheer enjoyment. Jonny leaped up and wrapped his legs around Trent's large ones, propped up to receive one of the most passionate French kisses of his life.

"Okay, you big distraction," Trent said, lowering Jonny to his bare feet. "Your turn. I'll help you take off some of the weights."

"How about all of them?" Jonny said with a laugh, having been nervous about doing squats at all.

"I know that you're not a pussy," Trent said offhandedly, removing two plates from his side.

Jonny did the same, realizing how heavy each plate was tonight.

Maybe I should have eaten that burger, he thought.

"Alright, I'm going to spot you on these," Trent said, one-hundred-thirty-five pounds left on the bar. "It might be heavy for you as a beginner, but I think with my help you'll be able to get it. We can adjust if need be after the first set. Plus, the safety guards are there on each side in case we fall."

God, I hope we do, Jonny wished to himself, getting into position beneath the bar. The pad was rougher than he thought it would be and the entire thing felt precarious, not to mention that he felt frail as fuck upon seeing his reflection, Trent's shoulders and outer thighs peeking out from either side.

"Now some things before we get going," Trent said, stepping closer and into his spotter's position. "This is dangerous, so I will stay close to you and the bar. Dump the bar off your back *only* as an absolute last resort, okay?"

It was hard for Jonny to concentrate, the smell and feel of Trent's hard muscles against his back while his dick was pointed down, nestled nicely between his cheeks.

"You get that?" Trent asked. "I need to hear you say it."

"Yes," Jonny replied meekly.

"Okay," Trent said, taking a single step back while lowering his hands by Jonny's waist. "Now lift."

Jonny pushed up, the weight now resting solely on his shoulders, the two stepped back from the assembly, where Jonny billowed like a stiff stick in the breeze.

"And down," Trent said, following Jonny as he squatted.

Jonny's legs buckled slightly as his thighs became parallel to the floor. Trent was quick to move, hands grasping Jonny's chest while his arms helped stabilize then lift him back to standing.

"Sorry," Jonny said nervously.

"No worries," Trent reassured him. "Let's try again."

Starting over, Jonny managed to plow through a good set of eight reps before his legs gave out. Walking slowly back to the rest position, they set the bar down, clanking, and Jonny relaxed.

"Holy moly," he said, "that was more intense than I thought."

"Agreed. Let's take the weights off so I can show you how to get better form and your ass to the grass so to speak."

With the plates gone, the bar only weighed forty-five pounds, which would be much more manageable for the remainder of the set. The two repositioned themselves to go through another set.

This time, Trent didn't step away, keeping himself planted firmly against Jonny. He hooked his arms beneath Jonny's armpits, grabbing hold of his pecs while his dick, still free and expectant, returned to its resting place down the center of Jonny's ass.

The two squatted together, reaching parallel then beyond, Jonny moaning as his ass neared the floor; the strain from the previous set starting to set his legs on fire. Making him feel even warmer, he could feel Trent's thick cock grinding against him, throbbing more powerfully as they repeated the process seven more times.

"Good boy," Trent muttered as they rested. "I think one more set should do it."

Jonny was aching, but also excited, his dick still rigid even after the leg curl incident.

Grabbing the bar, they both got into position. However, this time, as Jonny started his descent, Trent spat on his dick and pushed it all the way into Jonny's ass. They both bellowed, each sensation rivaling the other for superiority – Jonny's hole versus Trent's girth.

"Fuck, you're tight," Trent mumbled, breathing hard as he took the opportunity for a few lengthy strokes. "Oh shit, that feels good."

Jonny was unable to reply, ecstasy taking over through the combination of leg pain and his ass getting tore up by a nine by seven-inch rod.

"Alright Jonny-boy, it's time to squat. If my dick falls out of you, you're going to have to start that rep over again."

Jonny didn't mind if that meant more of this, but he went down slowly, making sure to stay filled the entire way down. At the bottom, Trent slid out ("Oh, fuck yeah!") then thrust himself back in a couple of times ("Take it, yeah all the way!"). Again and again, they squatted as Trent fucked, harder and harder until Jonny's legs were damn near breaking.

On the last rep, Trent kept Jonny locked in place, and he was unable to stand as Trent had his way with him, grunting and grinding until Jonny was nearly in tears from the pain and his ass reddened from being reamed.

With a great moan, Trent released him and Jonny shot up, stepping forward to rest on the bar. Trent didn't give him a second before he was on, then inside him again. His arms grasped Jonny's hips as he fucked, those huge nuts slapping against Jonny's skin.

Jonny had propped himself against the bar, watching himself heave and convulse in the mirror, sweat flowing down his entire body, joining ample amounts of precum as it all flicked off his bouncing dick against the glass.

God, it was a mess, and both men reveled in it.

"Fuck, Jonny-boy," Trent said, his stamina rising as more blood surged into his already swollen dick, screaming in near skin-splitting agony as he slid around inside Jonny's velvety asshole. "I'm not going to cum until I see you do…"

Jonny reached for his dick, Trent lashing a hand out to force him back to the bar.

"No hands!" he roared. "I'm gonna force it out of you."

"But I can't," Jonny pleaded, trying to glance over his shoulder to get a glimpse of Trent so he could beg him to stop... even though part of him didn't want to. "I've never...."

More precum splattered against the gym mirror, Jonny's cock saying that he damn well could.

"Look at your fucking self," Trent said, grabbing the back of Jonny's head and forcing him to look straight on again. "Stop doubting yourself and just... fucking... do it!"

Jonny oozed even more precum, long ropes of it helicoptering as his hard dick bounced around.

Trent was relentless, working himself up into a dripping fury. He continued rolling his hips, cock working overtime to bring every pleasurable sensation to Jonny that he could, while holding himself off from spilling over.

"Oh God..." Jonny muttered.

"Yeah, baby!"

"Oh God!"

"Come on!"

"OH GOD!"